As the Sun Goes Down: an anthology

by
Jay Howard

Published on behalf of Saluki Welfare Fund

Foreword

Thank you for buying this book and, in doing so, assisting the work of the Saluki Welfare Fund. This organisation is staffed entirely by volunteers, who strive to protect and re-home Salukis who fall on hard times. Such selfless endeavours restore my faith in humans. This is my small contribution to their efforts for these amazing sighthounds.

So, why did I choose this title? It's as the sun goes down, when the day's work is done, that I get a chance to write. These stories were written over many years, the inspiration coming from many unexpected sources. A hat in a charity shop led to Emily coming to live in my mind, an overheard conversation gave me as well as teacher Chris the inspiration we needed. Fragments of memories morph into skeletons onto which the tendon and muscle of pure flights of fancy can attach.

Maybe something in these stories will resonate with your own experiences. Maybe something you see or hear will lead to you writing a story of your own. Allow yourself the time to notice the small things in our lives, the funny, interesting, strange and downright peculiar things, and they will enrich you far more than money.

The evening is when I get a chance to read. Whenever your few well-earned 'me-time' minutes are, I hope you enjoy relaxing with your beverage of choice, dipping into this book to peek into the lives of the people who populate my imagination.

Jay Howard
February 2013

Salukis

Many years ago it was my privilege and honour to have two rescue Salukis sharing my life. I am not now in a position to give a couple of Salukis a safe place to live. I would dearly love to share my sofa - and my heart - with these very special sighthounds. I would at least like to be able to help fund the care they receive from the dedicated volunteers of the Saluki Welfare Fund. Alas, neither of these options is open to me at this time, but I live in hope.

In the meantime, I have used such skill as I have to compile this anthology. Every cent, every penny, will be paid over to the SWF. Thank you for choosing to help.

Please visit their website:

http://www.salukiwelfare.org.uk/index.shtml

Contents

Polly Polo

Hi Mum and Dad

Had to grab a few minutes to email you before I start work - give you a laugh to start the day. You'll not be surprised to learn that there is now one more person in the world convinced that your daughter is a total nutter. In fact, this morning I felt quite blonde. OK, I am blonde, but that's neither here nor there.

At 6:45, as I left for work, it was still hammering down and most of Chetmere Road was flooded. I drove along the middle of the road, grateful it's such a quiet rural road, and praying that there wouldn't be anyone coming the other way. Well, I was lucky – only one car to avoid at a point where it was only a minor wall of water whooshing up the side of Polly Polo. Such an elderly lady really shouldn't be taken out on a day like this, it's just not fair on her.

Anyway, for better or worse we were on our way.

Other parts of the road were totally flooded and there was

no option but to go through them. You've guessed it – the inevitable happened and Polly started struggling. She'd been very brave up to that point, gallant even, in her efforts to get me to work, but there is a limit to what you can ask an elderly car to cope with.

At first it was just fourth gear that didn't seem to be a very good idea. Then there was a bit of asthmatic wheezing on the hilly bits, a little bit of hesitation... She finally gasped to a halt at the main traffic lights at the bottom of Well Street, but we're used to that happening (that's the third time now) and good as gold she restarted. With a few extra revs we got across.

I'm now on Mount Street at the back of the shopping centre and had to stop for someone to cross at the lights. Oh dear...

So anyway, I now need my hazard warning lights on while I sort out this little problem of not restarting when I'm stuck at the pedestrian crossing. I know I must have hazard warning lights and I haven't got many buttons to choose from (two, actually) but it's still dark and I've never had to use them before. I got my torch out to thoroughly check the dash and eventually I located it. What a silly place to put a big button like that, right in the middle of the steering wheel where you're going to see it every day. I mean, it just becomes part of the furniture, doesn't it?

I'm now in a position to find the WD40 and give the fixing part of the plan a whirl. Good, found that. Even better I found the little levery thingy to release the bonnet. Now all I have to do is suss out how I opened the bonnet catch all those many months ago when Chris was showing me

Polly's guts (sounds like a nasty thing to do to a lady, really, but she seems to appreciate having her guts looked at occasionally).

Wow – I did well there – only a few minutes and the bonnet is standing up proud! Here we go with the spray – no, turn the can round so the spray sprays over Polly's electrics, not my hand.

Back in the car it's time to try again. Mmmmm.... loads of life in the battery but no hint of the engine firing. OK, give it a few minutes then try again. Still no sign of life. Try a few more times – still nothing. Now, I'm quite enjoying listening to Sarah Kennedy but I'm not clocked in to work yet and the minutes are ticking away. There's also a growing volume of traffic and I'm feeling decidedly in the way. Time for the breakdown call. The conversation went something like this...

"Good morning, how can I help you?"
"Good morning – I'm afraid my car doesn't like the rain, or rather she's had enough of going through flooded sections of road, and she's died."
"That's understandable on a day like this. Now, can I have your policy number?"

OK, so I got through the policy number and my name bit as it was written down on the card with the phone number (no, silly, the policy number, not my name) but then he asked for the number I was calling from. Now, I don't use my mobile very often. It took me two years to use the £20 pay as you go wotsit I put on it. How am I supposed to know my own number? I know I can get the phone to tell me what its number is, but not in the middle of a call.

"Don't worry," the very nice man said. He's one of those lovely people who manage to sound cheerful and helpful even when dealing with a hopeless case at that time in the morning. "I have caller display," he says. "Can you confirm your number?"

So he read it out to me, and it sounded sort of familiar, so we agreed that was my number.

"And what sort of car do you have?"
"A Vauxhall Polo."
"A Vauxhall Polo, Madam?"
"Yes, a blue one."
"Ermm… I realise the colour is important, but it doesn't really help at the moment. Is it a Vauxhall or is it a Polo?"
"Oh it's definitely a Polo – that's why her name is Polly – so that would make her… a, er… Volkswagen? Yes! That's it! A Volkswagen!"

Phew! Got past the hard part.

"Right, a VW Polo. And your registration?"
"I think it's J742 PPP. Do you want me to get out and check?"
"No, that's OK."

I think he was starting to lose the will to live at this stage but was still very cheerful. Was that suppressed chuckling I heard?

"And is it diesel or petrol?"
"Oh yes, it is."
"No, Madam, I need to know which it is – diesel or petrol?"
"Oh, sorry, it's petrol," I admitted sheepishly. "I'm afraid

my mind's not really on what we're doing, is it? I'm not very good with cars."

Mmmm – that was definitely chuckling I heard.

"That's quite all right."

We finally got through the bit about where I was (my mind momentarily went blank but luckily there's a street name sign right by that pedestrian crossing) and he advised me to give it 10 minutes to dry out, then try again. If there was still no joy he'd get someone straight out to me.

As you know I'm a bit of an impatient soul at times and only managed to wait for the time it took to eat a Werther's Original (and you know I can never just suck them). Joy of joys, she fired immediately! What a girl! So I phoned the nice man back.

"Thank you so much for your advice," says I. "Listen – she's running again!"
"Mmm, not quite there though," he tells me. "You need to rev the engine for a bit to dry it right out before you try and drive or it'll just die on you again."

So I put my foot down a bit. I wince when I put a strain on Polly: she deserves a little consideration in her old age.

"A bit more, Madam, just put your foot down a bit further for a while."
So I gritted my teeth and did as I was told. Sorry, Polly, I don't want to hurt you…

"That's better," the nice man said. "Just hold it there for a while then check everything's ticking over before trying driving."

"OK," I whimpered, "thank you for your help."

"No problem. You shouldn't need to, but if there are any more problems just call back."

He was right. I got into work OK, although I did panic a bit when I had to slow down and stop for a big artic in front of me that was inconsiderate enough to stop because he wanted to turn right.

I wonder...

will it be the same nice man on duty when I drive home?

Hope to see you Sunday
Lots of love
Julie xx

Emily's Hat

Traffic in the suburbs had been heavy and it was getting worse as Emily approached the city centre. She had been tempted to park up several miles back and find a bus to take her in the rest of the way, but her doubts about finding her way back had stopped her. Her smile was rueful as she remembered how easy it used to be to park up at their local station and get the train into the city. Now there were so few trains she'd never get back in time for the children.

At yet another set of red lights she reached round the back of her neck with one hand, trying to massage away the tension that had been growing with every mile she travelled further from her native fields and woodland.

She glanced over to the other lane, her attention drawn by the blare of the Rolling Stones hit that her daughter had listened to endlessly when it was released the previous summer. Alongside her was a very smart Mini, with an equally smart young woman at the wheel who was busy checking her heavy makeup in the mirror.

What is that song called? she thought, frowning as she tried to remember.

The word she heard at that point gave the answer - *Satisfaction*. She sincerely hoped she'd be able to satisfy Jon's expectations today.

She wriggled a little, unused to the feel of a skirt and tights, wishing they were her favourite old jeans, socks and wellies, and that she was mucking out the stables or gardening. She took a deep, steadying breath and gently rotated her head, admitting that it had to be today, so she'd best just get on with it. No more procrastination: this really was her last chance before she and Jon travelled south for the sales conference and the concomitant entertainment. Emily wasn't quite sure which facet of all this was most frightening. All she knew for sure was that the first of her many fears and worries had to be overcome today – the purchase of a suitable outfit.

Emily parked up in the multi-storey and made her way through the busy streets to the department store. She stood on the kerb and gathered her courage around her, but it felt more of a wet paper bag than protective armour. Her mind drifted back to the previous Friday.

"There you go, love," he'd said, leaning over to kiss her forehead.

She'd been sat in her favourite armchair, mending a light cotton blouse that would soon be needed in the growing heat of the new season. He'd taken the sewing out of her hands and replaced it with a white envelope, obviously a card.

"What's this? My birthday's not for another month yet."

His lovable boyish grin told her how pleased he was with himself, his startling blue eyes sparking sapphire lights.

"I know that. This is extra." He sat on the padded arm of the chair and draped his arm across her shoulders. "I stopped off on the way home," he said. "Go on, open it up!"

She took the card out and paused, admiring the beautiful red rose on the front. She looked up at him, took his hand and kissed the palm.

"Open it!"

The sheet of paper within gave details of a store account. The spending limit left her eyes wide and mouth open.

"But -"

"But nothing. I'm not having you wearing that charity shop hat and the outfit from last year's wedding. You're the wife of the Sales and Marketing Manager (UK) now and need to look the part next Thursday."

"Well, I could maybe get some new shoes," she said, thinking about what else could be done with that much money.

"You could maybe do as I ask and buy the whole kit and caboodle." His slight frown warned he'd brook no argument on this. "I can afford it now I've been promoted. The standard farmer's wife fashion of these parts is just not good enough, Emily. I don't want their pitying glances if you look any less than perfect."

Her head snapped back from the verbal slap, her sharply indrawn breath was loud.

Has he been ashamed of me all this time?

A sudden solitary tear shimmered in the corner of her eye, her pleasure in the card gone. He was instantly apologetic, gathering her into his arms and kissing her hair.

"Emily, I'm so sorry, that came out all wrong. You always look beautiful to me, whatever you're wearing. Honestly, I just thought I was helping, please don't cry."

She pulled him tight and spoke into his waist. "You have, my love, and I do appreciate it, really. I'll go in next week."

He laughed, the sound a little forced. "Well, the week after won't be much use." He tipped up her face with cupped fingers under her chin, wiping his thumb across her cheek. "You are allowed to enjoy spending on yourself, you know."

She nodded and forced a smile.

Now it was next week. He'd removed the 'where' part of the equation. She had sorted out the 'how'. Now she had to sort out the 'what'.

She dragged her eyes down from the fancy gold lettering on bottle green above the entrance, By Appointment to Her Majesty Queen Elizabeth no less, and hesitantly advanced to the door.

All that money to be squandered on one outfit! It feels vaguely obscene.

"Good morning, Madam," the uniformed doorman greeted her, ushering her in with a smile and a tip of his hat.

No backsliding now, Emily, she told herself sternly. *You'll look a right fool if you turn and run. And Jon will never forgive you if you fall at this hurdle.*

She knew Jon loved her, as she loved him. She was very proud of the hard work and dedication that had seen him rise through the ranks. But she also knew how their life together had started. She could clearly remember how flattered (and surprised!) she had been to find herself being wooed by Jon, the most handsome and extrovert of that year's intake of trainee sales reps.

Emily's habit had always been to rush back to her parents' farm after work, never stopping to socialise with any of her colleagues. She was the one they called Mouse Clarke instead of Miss Clarke. She was the one people assumed must have been at the meeting because the minutes always appeared promptly, but no-one could ever recall actually seeing her there. Her face and figure were comely enough, but she just lacked that certain flair and self-confidence that other women had.

What Emily didn't know, until it was too late, was that Jon's peers had bet him a night's drinks that his newly honed sales patter would not be good enough to sell himself to her as far as agreement to a date. Mouse Clarke never dated, period.

Strangely enough, that first date had been a resounding

success. They had found their views on so many aspects of life were in accord, and had talked most of the night away. Jon had insisted on a second date, then a third. Within six weeks they were an acknowledged item, engaged within six months. Now, after nine years of marriage, Emily was blissfully happy caring for Jon and their two children, totally immersed in their lives and that of the village. But she could no longer sidestep Jon's need for her to get more involved in his work. She had to accept the social duties that went along with his promotion.

I wish it still only meant hosting dinner parties for him.

"Can I be of some assistance, Madam?"

Startled, Emily realised she had been lost in reverie in front of the same display for several minutes.

"Yes, I, um, need an outfit," she stammered.

Oh Lord, why do even the assistants look smarter than me? And I took such care with my appearance this morning. I guess Jon's right about me needing a new outfit.

"Yes, Madam. Would this be for a special occasion?"

Emily could hear the undercurrent of mockery in the voice. If someone who looked like her came into this very exclusive establishment for an outfit it had to be for a one-off 'special occasion', not something one did routinely as part of a pampered, hedonistic lifestyle.

"Yes, it's for Ladies' Day. That's Royal Ascot, you know."

"Yes, Madam."

The smirk was almost visible and Emily blushed furiously.

Of course she knows about Ladies' Day, one of the days of the social calendar.

She kept her eyes on the floor while her body was appraised, biting on the inside of her lip.

The assistant led Emily to the changing rooms, on the

way selecting a suit and two dresses for her to try. Emily felt like she was being taken to the Headmistress's room for punishment, but quickly changed her mind.

The changing room was actually a very pleasant place to be on such a hot day, with its air conditioning and subtle lighting. There was plenty of room, and it was an actual room, no worrying about curtains that didn't quite meet the cubicle edge, and the mirrors showed Emily how well her active life had kept her in trim. She could feel the quality of the clothes as they slipped over her skin and settled naturally into place, with no awkward tugging needed against poor cuts and slipshod sewing.

But how can I choose the best option when I've no mental yardstick to check them against?

She tried each of them on three times and was still unsure. Each time her assistant had carefully brushed imaginary creases out of the clothes as she returned them to their hangers, with no sign of impatience when they were requested again.

Emily could feel herself getting more and more flustered but eventually, with subtle guidance, she made her selection. The assistant smiled a cat's-got-the-cream smile and turned to leave the changing rooms with the citrus lemon and cream dress over her arm.

"No, wait," Emily called, one hand raised and panic in her eyes.

The assistant looked back, swivelling on her heel, one finely-plucked eyebrow raised. "Madam?"

"I, er..." She lowered her hand. "Are you sure?"

It was not a colour in which one could blend into the background.

"It is by far the best dress for your colouring. You've seen how well it complements your skin tone, and your hair - it brings out all those wonderful burnished copper depths."

"It does fit well," Emily conceded.

"The fit is superb. There's no-one it would look better on."

Emily meekly followed her.

The assistant stroked the dress into a box, seeming reluctant to let it out of the store. She glanced up at Emily from under thickly mascaraed eyelashes and sighed.

Does she think I'm not 'worthy' of it? Emily thought, suddenly feeling more cross than nervous.

"Might I suggest Madam visits our millinery department next?" the assistant prompted after reverently consigning the boxed dress to its store bag. "It is rather de rigueur to have a hat for Ladies' Day."

There's that damn smirk back again!

"Of course I'm getting a hat!" Emily snapped. *Jon's money is as good as anyone else's. Of course I deserve the dress. This is all getting just too much, and I'm still only half way to my goal.*

-0-

Sat in front of the mirror, Emily could not help but let her eyes slide sideways to watch two very fashionable young women who were trying on hat after hat for the sheer pleasure of it.

How do they manage to make an apparently simple hat look so chic just by casually giving it a little tilt? How do they get away with creating such chaos while the assistant looks flustered and harried, not them?

"If I may see the dress, Madam, to ensure we match the exact shade of cream?" her assistant suggested.

"Of course... I'll just..."

The assistant smoothly took over the opening of the box

from Emily's fumbling fingers. Emily bit her lip at the surprise evident in the assistant's face when the startling yellow fairly leapt out at them.

"A most interesting choice, Madam."

Why didn't I go with my instincts and settle on the navy suit? It's too late now: there's no way I can face that snotty assistant again to change it.

The new assistant held the dress up against Emily and nodded, a smile of amazed approval curving her lips. "I believe a hat with a wide brim would be best. One moment, please, and I'll fetch the one that I'm sure will be absolutely perfect for Madam. It came in just this morning."

I don't care if it's the ugliest hat in the world. I'm not a hat person. I hate hats! Just let me buy it and end this agony. I want to go home...

The hat was indeed perfect, and Emily found that she, too, was now smiling. Could she really pull this off?

"I'll bet it was Nadine who assisted you with the dress purchase," her new assistant said while helping Emily learn how to put the hat on to best effect. "She is totally amazing, spots possibilities no-one else would."

Emily's panic flared again. "I won't look odd or strange, will I? Why would no-one else choose that dress?"

"You'll look totally stunning, in all the best ways."

"Is it possible…" Emily paused, her eyes pleading, "Could you help me with the shoes and bag?"

"I'd love to help you."

-0-

"Are you ready, love?" Jon asked.

Emily took one last look in the cheval mirror in their hotel bedroom and gave the hat what she hoped was the same little tilt that she had seen could be so effective. Nervously she turned round and was reassured by Jon's smile and the love in his eyes.

"You look absolutely gorgeous, darling. You'll knock them all dead and the folks back home will see you in tomorrow's papers, headline blaring 'Unknown beauty takes Ascot by storm'."

Bless him, but why didn't I buy the navy? Such a nice, safe colour, and so serviceable.

They shared the stretched limo with two other managers and their girlfriends.

Strange... From what Jon's said I could have sworn they were both married. Obviously I'm more out of touch with his work and colleagues than I realised. They seem nice enough, though.

She reminded herself that today she was expected to join in the conversation and 'fun', and must not allow her instinct to fade into the background get the better of her.

Not that I've got much option about being noticed, wearing this beacon of a dress.

As Jon handed her out of the limo she blushed at the very obvious stares from a group of men who were passing by. She tilted her head away from them and suddenly realised the advantage of a hat with a brim. She could use it to allow people to see her face, or hide from them entirely. It didn't matter a jot that she was so noticeable in the citrus yellow. She could choose to accept or reject such attention. Hold her head this way and it was an invitation, hold it that way and it was a dismissal. She could be as friendly or rude as she liked without saying a word.

That was why Regency and Edwardian ladies depended on their exquisite fans, not for a cooling movement of air but for the language the fans spoke in skilful hands. Well, I don't have a fan but I do have a hat and I'm going to use it for all it's worth!

A feeling of warm affection for her hat started to grow. Emily glanced up at Jon from beneath the brim as she straightened up and pushed the car door shut behind her.

How sensuous that feels, how coy and flirtatious! With my hat I can be whoever I wish to be, in this place where I know no one and no one knows me.

They entered the hospitality area, the entry corridor mirrored on both walls. Her eyes sparkled as she saw the confirmation in her reflections that she looked her very best. The dress fitted superbly and even the tilt of the hat was just right.

Waiters were ready with trays laden with champagne and she graciously inclined her head in thanks, feeling quite regal. They walked towards the huge windows overlooking the course and she heard a low wolf whistle just behind her. She felt a blush burn her cheeks but felt safe from comment within the privacy of her hat.

Jon's colleagues seemed more interested in checking out the women inside than looking at the action outside. Their girlfriends chattered on nonstop about the latest celebrity gossip, equally uninterested in the horses and people. It became just background babble to her ears as she watched the fascinating kaleidoscope of action around the course and stands.

"All right, love?" Jon asked and squeezed her hand.

Emily turned to him, that he might see the love for him in her eyes and her delight at the day on her face. She squeezed his hand back and sipped her champagne, smiling at the prospect of the role she was about to play.

How surprised he will be!

"Well, gentlemen," she announced, "if you've quite finished checking out the form of the fillies at the bar I suggest we go and assess some horseflesh."

Emily confidently led the way without waiting for a reply, somehow knowing that today she would be the one followed rather than the follower.

Close up, the thoroughbreds really were magnificent, silken ripples of light flowing over well-proportioned bone and finely honed muscle. It was evident the stable lads had been determined that their charges should look their best for this magnificent occasion and the horses had picked up the electric excitement in the air, skittering on their still tight lead reins. Emily was discussing which horse to bet on when a touch on her elbow announced the MD's arrival.

"Emily, my dear, how nice to see you looking so well," he greeted her with a kiss on the cheek. "May I present His Highness Sheikh Abdul ibn Kefirat? He wished to be introduced to the most stunning woman here and was most disappointed when I mentioned that our newest European manager had already snapped her up."

"George, it's been far too long since you came to dinner – phone me when we get back home." She turned to the Sheikh and shook his proffered hand. "I'm honoured to make your acquaintance, Your Highness. I've heard a great deal about you."

"I want to know why I cannot say likewise."

He has a most charming smile.

"I overheard some of your conversation, Emily. You seem very knowledgeable about horses. Do you often attend the racing?"

"Indeed no! This is the first time and I have yet to discover how one goes about placing a bet."

"Then what is the source of this knowledge of horses?"

"Your Highness -"

"Abdul, please," he interrupted.

"I am sure," she paused and smiled, "Abdul, that you know the ancient Arabic story of Amr?"

29

Abdul slightly raised one dark eyebrow, his near-black eyes giving nothing away.

"Amr asked his cousin to buy him a horse. Muslim protested that he knew nothing about horses, to which Amr replied, 'Are you not a hunting man?' 'Yes,' he replied. 'Then look for everything which you consider good in the hound and seek it in the horse.' And Muslim bought for Amr a horse the like of which had never been seen by the Bedouin Arabs." Emily gestured gracefully towards the ring. "The thoroughbreds we see before us are descendants of such Arab horses."

"Bravo, Emily!" He applauded gently. "And which hounds do you know so well?"

"I have the privilege of being the carer of two Salukis, Sabbah, the morning, and La'aman, flash of light. Mine are rescue Salukis whom I named after two very fine champions in British breeding history."

Abdul bowed to her. "Jon, you have been munificently blessed by Allah. Guard your wife and your hounds well. So, Emily, what is your choice for the 3:30?"

Emily was prompt in her reply. "Firestorm."

"And what points of the hound do you see in the horse that make you so positive?"

This is fun! I might come racing again.

They discussed equine anatomy for several minutes before Abdul excused himself to return to his guests.

"Do you realise whose horse you picked?" Jon asked as he led Emily towards the bookies. He could see from her innocent expression that she did not. "Abdul's. Feel's strange calling him that. He owns many of the horses here this week, of course, but Firestorm is said to be his favourite."

"Then let us hope, for his sake as well as ours, that he wins."

They took their betting slips and collected yet more champagne in readiness to shout Firestorm to victory.

-0-

Later, much later, Emily gratefully kicked off her shoes and threw the hat on the bed.

What a day!

Jon put his arms round her waist from behind and nuzzled her neck.

"You were amazing!" he congratulated her. "The MD reckons I'll go far with a wife like you behind me."

"Oh, Jon, I love you and I'm so pleased I didn't let you down. But it didn't feel like it was me there. Sometimes it was as though I was standing just to one side listening to this sparkling, witty conversationalist I'd only just met."

Jon smiled his endearing boy-grin that Emily hadn't seen during the many months while he was trying to prove himself worthy of promotion.

"Don't you remember, when we first met, how many mornings we both needed matchsticks to keep our eyes open after yet again talking the night away?" he asked gently.

"I remember." She turned in his arms and rested her head on his shoulder. "But that was just the two of us. I've never been able to join in groups like that."

"Well maybe it was you, and maybe it wasn't, or maybe you were just talking out of your hat."

How well you know me, my darling. I think I may have to buy a few more hats.

~~~

Simile and Metaphor

I was never quite sure if they subconsciously thought that a conversation couldn't be overhead by other people if they were huddled in a small group, or if they thought teachers were deaf, or if they really wanted us to overhear what they had to say. Wouldn't say it to my face, I suppose, so it was a way of getting their complaints across. Or maybe they wanted to emphasise I was one of the opposition. Us and Them.

Whatever, I wasn't in the mood for it, not to hear in passing, "Oh, God, she's in today! I was hoping she'd been run over by a bus or come down with something nice like rabies."

They were in my last class of the day and obviously looking forward to it with the same anticipation I was. I didn't need them to tell me they found the weekly assignment boring. I'd read enough of their submissions to get the general drift.

There was a host of topics I would rather have covered, or covered the ones we were given in a different way, but there was the little matter of a syllabus to cover. 'The student must demonstrate…'

I felt stifled, never mind them.

Every week I heard the moans and groans, knowing full well that I'd make an equivalent groan for each and every one of them when it came to marking their work. I'd never imagined, in my youthful enthusiasm, that it would all boil down to obeying the edicts of the bureaucrats who had probably never taught in their lives, leavened with the growing mountain of admin every time some bright spark had another cracking idea to make the statistics look good. Theirs or ours?

My pressing problem of the moment, as we all headed off to lunch, was that particular group's weekly assignment, had they but known it. They didn't want to do it, but I hadn't even written it yet, and the clock was ticking inexorably. Yes, I had a stock of 'suitable' assignments, handed down teacher to teacher, year to year, that could be adapted as necessary, but I was as desperate to capture their interest as they were to be interested. However, I'd met the stage before any writer's block they might experience. I'd met the barrier of a blank mind for even setting the assignment they were to write about.

I could feel the frown lines becoming permanent. I'd look awful long before I got to retirement at this rate.

First things first. At least I could be sure of achieving something positive today if I nipped into town now and got all the bits and pieces I needed instead of having to make a special trip in on Saturday. Weekends were all too short as it was. Not having a proper lunch break would do nothing to improve my temper by the time I stood in front of Biko group but they'd have to put up with it.

Biko group! We were no longer allowed to use A to D to distinguish between the groups in case the little lovelies got a complex about not being A graded. The very concept of streaming was anathema in today's political climate. This group was supposedly named for Steve Biko but they're not stupid – they were still aware that they were the B group, capable but not the best.

The town was extra crowded as it was market day. I love ambling through a good street market, trying to spot the special bargain or that unusual item you can never find in the shops. Even without making a purchase the banter with the stallholders was fun. I hated rushing around like this. 'Extra hour in bed,' I repeated to myself on a loop, like a mantra.

Last stop – there'd just about be time. I made my selections at top speed (never mind the differences between the brands – that shoe polish was the right colour, those laces the right length) and stood fuming at the counter while both assistants took forever to serve the woman ahead of me, more interested in their own conversation than in doing the job they were being paid for.

Come on! I'm going to be late at this rate!

I was still guaranteed to be back in class before the last of the stragglers of Biko, though. I'd love to be able to exclude late students, they were so disruptive for the rest of the group, but that was yet another practice that was not allowed now. We are totally hog-tied when it comes to enforcement of discipline. However, it is increasingly easy to find ourselves being disciplined.

My temper was fraying rapidly under the influence of such bleak feelings of impotence, but suddenly my attention was brought back to the present location. The assistants, bless them, solved one of my problems without ever knowing it. Perhaps I should make it a habit to listen in to other people's conversations?

Biko group settled much more quickly than usual. Children, and I still consider them to be children at fifteen, even though I try to treat them as the adults they think they are, are very quick to pick up on other people's moods. They don't often let on, they just use this knowledge to their own advantage. Today they sensed something was different while I stood at the whiteboard. I hate that I can't use blackboards and chalk any more: apparently it can be construed as 'racist'. So why is 'whiteboard' not racist? Black and white are colours that relate to more than just skin colour. Will it become an offence to use the word 'black' unless you actually are? Anyway, I wrote on it 'He hadn't got the sense of a shovel'. That puzzled them a bit!

"OK," I turned back to face them. "Today I am scheduled to check your knowledge and understanding of simile and metaphor, a subject that I know has really captured your imagination."

Pause to allow the expected griping to die down.

"While I was shopping today – quiet, Richard: it has been known for the male of the species to shop as well – I overheard two assistants talking. One of them said, 'He was trying to force his foot into the display size 8 shoe and I know he's got size 10 feet. Some people haven't got the sense of a shovel.'"

Pause again. Let them try and suss out where we're going with this.

"I can see you don't have a problem with this expression. It is very vibrant, very evocative. But think about it for a moment. It brings together the animate 'sense' with the inanimate 'shovel'. On its own level it works, but why? Who said it first? Why was it remembered? Who said it this time?"

Good, I've got their attention, at least for a while.

"Was it someone of your generation or someone middle-aged whom I overheard? Let's have a show of hands on this. First, hands up if you think it was someone young who said it."

Quick count, write it on the board, deduct that figure from the class attendance of the day (never the same as the number of names on the register, especially on a Friday afternoon) and write that down for the middle-aged figure.

"Aw, Miss, I didn't get to vote!" John complained loudly.

"Perhaps because I don't want certain members of this

36

group double voting, John. Anyone want to change their vote? No? Right, let's proceed.

"What I want you to discuss this afternoon is the usage of simile and metaphor among your generation in comparison with how it was used by your parents. English is a living, constantly changing language. What kind of things do you say that your parents wouldn't, and vice versa? There was no hesitation in your voting just now – why was that?"

Blank looks – bring it back to specifics.

"Make a start with 'sense of a shovel'. Is it simile or metaphor? How and why does it work so well? Does it only work verbally or would it work in print too? Is its usage just related to age or does class come into it? OK, OK! Before you all jump on me I know we're supposed to be a classless society now. Let me rephrase this. Do poorly educated people express themselves in the same way that, say, university graduates do?

"Form whatever groups you feel comfortable with for this discussion. You have twenty minutes left for it. I suggest you note down some of the ideas your group comes up with because your assignment is to give me a reasoned presentation of your group's conclusions. Specifically, I want one thousand words on the usage of simile and metaphor, with reference to socio-economic groups and comparing contemporary and historical usage. Yes, Richard, I will write it on the board."

I hoped it would be a noisy session, from debate not complaints. I also hoped the adjoining classes' teachers wouldn't complain.

-0-

I was very pleased that, after the inevitable exaggerated

scraping and banging as they sorted themselves out, five roughly equal-sized groups had formed and eventually the chatter did actually settle down, after several promptings, to the matter in hand. In fact, it got quite heated over in one corner. It was going to be a hard act to follow. I took the opportunity to write the assignment on the board. 'Compare and contrast, with examples, the usage of simile and metaphor among your own generation and that of your parents. Additional marks will be awarded for a discussion of the effects of socio-economic status.'

"Miss!"

I didn't need to turn round to recognise it was John again, ever the most vocal of the group.

"We can't agree if it's a simile or a metaphor."

Was it worth making the point once again?

"John, have you ever considered that at the end of this academic year you won't be here in class for me to answer all your questions? Try to think independently and find your own solutions to problems."

"But, Miss, won't you -"

"Yes, I know." It was always the same. "'Just this once', eh, John? I have checked the class dictionary, which as usual is on the shelf at the back. It not only gives very clear definitions of simile and metaphor but also gives excellent examples. I suggest you also refer back to your notes from earlier lessons this week."

There were grumblings but they did retrieve the dictionary.

"And before you ask, the spellings are on the board."

I returned to the board to pre-empt the next complaints and listed the various points I had suggested they cover in their analysis. Hopefully they would find themselves with understanding and patient managers in the workplace that was so soon to replace the life at school where mental idleness seemed accepted as the norm.

For once the lesson seemed to pass quickly for all of us. The discussions were continuing even as the bell rang. They were eager to force their opinions onto group consciousness and acceptance and amazingly I had to chivvy the last stragglers out of the door. I felt very satisfied as I gathered my belongings and followed them out.

"You're looking very pleased with yourself, Chris," Helen called over the intervening car as we prepared to go home. "Got that Friday feeling?"

"Oh yes! A good Friday, the weekend ahead, and for once I'm looking forward to some assignments to mark."

"You'd better watch out," Helen said and laughed. "They'll be dusting off the straightjackets if they hear members of staff coming out with heresy like that."

It was actually true, though. For once I was looking forward to the possibility that my students might teach me a thing or two about the language I love, approaching the subject as they were with the very different perspective and insights from another generation. Perhaps this time I wouldn't have to hand too many of them back marked R (referred) and have them resubmitted time and again until they got the extra marks needed to get past the grading of 'Not yet passed'. We can't ever tell them they've failed, oh no!

Yes, I was feeling good. Hope springs eternal.

~~~

Jackie's Bike

I realised from an early age what the differences are between being one of a large brood and being an only child.

Jackie says to me, "You're the lucky ones. You've always got someone to play with or go out with. I get awful lonely and Mam keeps me home all the time 'cos she's scared of what might happen if I'm out by myself."

I told her it was 'cos she hasn't got the brains she was born with, well that's what me Da says any road. I says to her, "I wouldn't mind a bit of peace and quiet. I'm sick of all the fights and taking care of the young 'uns, and another set of nappies every year."

She doesn't have to eat as fast as she can to be first to get to the seconds. And I know she doesn't have to help out with the chores. Her Mam can cope by herself, with there only being the three of them.

Now don't get me wrong, I do love my family, all of them, even little Jason, never mind there's always a bogey hanging from his nose - why won't he blow his nose like I tell him to? And Mam and Da are the best in the world. Mam's so big and strong she can lift a sack of coal in each hand and lug them indoors, no sweat. Da's real small, but wiry. In the war his mates called him the The Little Corporal, like that Hitler bloke. I asked him didn't he mind, and he just said he was a Corporal and he is little, so what's to get annoyed about? He's nothing like Hitler, though, he's smashing, my Da is. He always has a big grin when he sees us and swoops us up in the air, swinging us round till we shout, "Enough!"

Yes, we always have a laugh with Da. And I have to giggle when Mam and Da go out: from behind they look like Laurel and Hardy. But by, they do look smart when they go to the Social on special nights, like the Coronation. I feel right proud of them.

Where was I? Oh, yes. Most of all, though, Jackie doesn't have to wait her turn for the toy pot. If she wants something she just looks pleadingly at her Da with those big blue eyes of hers, and all that long blonde hair that stays properly curled all day, and whatever she asks for, her Da rushes out to get it for his 'little princess'.

It's not like that for us. Every Friday we have the ritual of the pay packet. Da gets home at the end of the week, tired but still keen to get out to his allotment. He wipes his mouth after his supper and that's the signal for Mam to sit down with him, a cup of tea each, and cluster the pots on the table between them. Da then does this big ceremony, handing over his pay packet to Mam with a pretend trumpet fanfare and a sly wink to us, which makes us giggle. She carefully checks it, always the full amount minus the one pint Da allows himself with his mates on the way home from work, and we watch. It's awesome, seeing so much money all at once. Imagine what I'll be able to buy when I get a job and have that much every week!

The pots are opened then to receive their weekly addition. There's the rent pot, the electric pot, the gas pot, the food pot. There's the bright red clothes pot and its paler cousin, the shoes pot. But the pot of most interest to us, which unfortunately always receives the smallest share, is the emerald green toy pot. I love that colour! It's the exact richness of the moss in the woods that's so soft against my cheek when I'm resting on a hot summer day, with just the rustling leaves and birdsong instead of the noise and busyness of home.

Now, the toy pot isn't for birthdays and Christmas. Once Mam's pots have swallowed their weekly share the rest of the money is handed back to Da. He takes it to their bedroom where he has his own pots, pots we're not supposed to know about. He keeps the birthdays pot and the Christmas pot, the holiday pot and the one he keeps best hidden of all, the pot for gifts for Mam. The toy pot downstairs is for 'extras' for us children. We have to take turns for that money. We ask for crayons and paper, or canes and tissue paper to make a kite, or plasticine, or a new ball, and then have to wait, jealously guarding the sequence of its emptying. My brothers will nip in, quick as wink, and take my turn if I don't watch out.

It was my turn next for the toy pot when Jackie got her bike, the first on the street that was brand new and a girl's bike to boot, no crossbar getting in the way, so your dress can hang down properly, not get hitched up showing your knickers to the boys if you're not careful. I changed my request from Ivanhoe to a bike - well, you won't get if you don't ask - but I wasn't surprised when Mam just laughed.

Jackie called over the fence for my older sister, Sarah, to go and have a look, and Mam insisted she let me tag along. I think Mam just wanted me out from under her feet while she was baking. I love a lick of the mixing bowl after the cake has gone in the oven, and Mam says my eyes make her feel guilty if she doesn't leave an extra bit for me.

Jackie wouldn't let me touch her wonderful bike in case I left dirty fingerprints on it. Everyone knows if there's a way of getting dirty I've already found it. Miss Jackson won't let me take my turn as ink monitor at school now, not since I 'accidentally' missed the ink well and splashed it all over Stephen, and his new exercise book. I got it splashed all over my dress too but that was a small price to pay to get back at the monster who pulls my hair and calls me names. How I long for short hair and the right to fight like the boys do. I'd give him what for, and no mistake, but I don't want detention.

Jackie's bike is pink, which is yuk, but looks very big and powerful. It has three gears and shiny wheel spokes, which glinted the sun back at me when I saw it. I could imagine the wheels whirling round, faster and faster, spinning the sunlight back at plodding pedestrians as I flashed past them on my way to adventure. Jackie showed Sarah how well she could ride it up and down the street, and even let Sarah have a go, squealing in terror until she learned to control it. I didn't know what all the fuss was about – you pedalled to go forwards and had brakes to stop. What could be so hard about that?

"It's so difficult to get your balance at first!" Sarah said, and giggled, all girly.

Well, it would be if you're not in the habit of playing the games Jack and I play when Mam isn't checking to see I'm not behaving like a tomboy again. Proper games, boys' games, need physical daring, strength and balance. I just had to have a go and show them how to really ride a bike.

How though? They weren't going to give me a chance so I'd have to just grab one. I was determined, so I started the watching and waiting game. I was very lucky actually. It felt like forever at the time but it was really less than a fortnight before Jackie was getting bored with her bike. It was always the way with Jackie. Mam said that it was because she got things too easily so she didn't appreciate what she had.

Jackie had proudly paraded her bike around and made sure everyone on the street had admired it, but now she was back to sitting on the kerb with Sarah, playing with their dolls that they claimed were actors in the plays they made up. And while they did that the bike was left unnoticed on the pavement behind them. It was another hot, drowsy afternoon and most people were sticking to shady spots, so there was no one close enough to stop me. I carefully, oh so quietly, lifted the bike upright and straddled it, and settled my hands round the rubber handlebar grips. Carefully I got the pedal in the right position, as I'd seen Jackie do it, weight on it, lift into the saddle and off! It was a jarring bump from the pavement down the kerb to the road (Jackie always started with it on the road, of course) but somehow I kept it upright. I was cycling!

I ignored the shouts behind me to stop. Not for me the careful turning at the corner to come back down our street. There was a whole wide world out there I could get to before teatime with the speed of a bike beneath me! The wind of my own passing blew my hair streaming behind me. I couldn't help but laugh out loud. It was glorious! The pedals turned faster and faster without any real effort at all, especially when I figured out how to change gear. My legs were tireless and would take me to the ends of the earth. I was flying! The familiar streets had passed in a flash and I was in virgin territory. I was an explorer, as brave as Livingstone!

But reality hit, quite literally. You see, I didn't know about Lea Hill. I do now. Lea Hill is steep – very steep. And at the bottom of this steep hill is a crossroads which is very busy when the factories empty and all the workers head for home. There seemed a solid mass of buses, cars and bikes and I was heading straight for them! What was it Jackie had said about the brakes? Was it front first and then back, or back first and then front? Oh, God! Help me – I can't remember!

I slammed them both on with eyes shut tight.

-0-

I woke in hospital to find a heavy plaster cast on my right arm and Mam looking very worried beside my bed.

"Jane! Thank God you've woken!"

Mum scooped me into a huge cuddle, tears streaming down her face.

"Why are we here, Mam?"

Whoops – shouldn't have said that perhaps.

"Why? You ask me why? When, oh when, will you learn? We've been worried sick about you! You could have been killed! Concussion, broken arm, and you ask me why?"

That was it – the sobs started in earnest.

"I'm OK, Mam, honest. It doesn't hurt…" I had a stinking headache but I wasn't about to admit to that.

Mam insisted on taking me straight home to look after me. A pity, really, as it looked like it could have been quite good fun in the hospital. It was nice, though, to be the centre of attention back home. Everyone called to see how I was and to hear my story. Mam made up a bed for me on the settee so that she could keep an eye on me. The doctor had carefully instructed her on what to look out for as a possible complication of a concussion, whatever that was.

I felt right bad when Jackie came round, half carrying her bike with its squashed up front wheel from when I crashed through the hedge. She stopped and looked at me through the living room window and I thought she was going to cry. I went out to the back yard and Da was on one knee checking it out while Jackie held it upright. They both looked at me and Da looked so disappointed with me I thought I was going to cry. I bit inside my bottom lip, hard, to stop myself.

"I'm so sorry, Jackie," I says. "I never meant to damage it." And she looks at me, all angry like.

"There's many things happen in life that we don't

intend," says Da. "Some things we can't avoid, and some things we should have made sure didn't happen in the first place. This shouldn't have happened, should it, Jane?"

I couldn't look him in the eye so I looked at my feet. "No, Da."

"This time I can put it right for you. There'll be times when I won't be there to sort it out for you, so think on," he says. "Think before you act in future."

Mam saved me that time. "Get back in here!" she shouts at me from the scullery. "I won't have you passing out and cracking your head on those cobbles. Stay on that settee like you were told until you're told different." Suited me as I didn't know what else to say to Jackie to make it right and stop Da looking at me like that.

Jackie forgave me when Da told her he could fix the wheel, and she came in each day with games to play with me while I was kept on the settee. Loads of people came to see me and they'd gasp and be amazed when I told my story. Two days it was before the doc called and said I was well enough to use my own bed again. Before that happened, though, I'd overheard something very exciting!

Mam and Da thought I was sound asleep, but it was very difficult to do more than doze on that settee, especially when you wanted to scratch the bit of your arm you couldn't reach because of the plaster cast. I made do with scratching off a scab on my knee instead.

"You realise we're going to have to get her a bike," Mam said to Da.

"It's ages yet to her birthday or Christmas and we don't normally go that far from the toy pot." I could hear in Da's voice he was very dubious. "We don't want the children to get the wrong idea, do we, love? She did wrong and shouldn't be rewarded for it."

"I know, I know. But I also know that if she doesn't

have her own bike Jane's going to go out and 'borrow' any bike she can find. You heard her describing to the others the feeling of freedom, of 'flying' on a bike. She's hooked and wants more of that feeling. We can't stop her. We'll get abject apologies afterwards but you know what she's like, it won't stop her doing it anyway. All we can do is try to ensure that she's on a bike that's small enough for her to control."

"Aye, love, happen you're right. I'll ask around the lads and see what I can find. But she's going to have to do more than apologise to Jackie. It's taken me a lot of time to repair the front wheel of that bike."

"I suppose we could make her go round every week to clean Bill's car and Jackie's bike. She's a practical-minded lass and a practical punishment will get through to her best."

The ritual of the pay packet had a special significance for me then. Each week I listened carefully when it came to the toy pot. The passing of six weeks was marked by the removal of the plaster cast but still nothing happened. Then, at last, the loose change clanged onto the bare bottom of the pot. That meant only one thing – it had been emptied for a purchase! It was so difficult to sleep that night but extra toys were never given until Saturday morning. In fact, they were liable to not appear at all if we didn't behave ourselves.

Saturday dawned chilly but bright, the scent of autumn in the air. Under Mam's watchful eye I had to eat my breakfast even though my stomach churned. I forced the last spoonful of cereal down my protesting throat and returned the spoon to the bowl.

"Now, Mam?"

"Yes, love. Out you go!"

Da was stood there in the yard waiting for me, holding

the bike – my bike. It was quite perfect. Oh, I know it wasn't a new one or anything like as flash as Jackie's bike. But hers was pink. Dad had painted mine a glossy, glorious emerald green.

"Thank you, Da!" I managed to whisper. I was so glad that the one thing that was never rationed or on a rota in our house was love.

~~~

Out The Other Side

Sophie hesitated, needle part way through the denims she was mending for her son. She tried to gauge from her husband's expression if this was a good time to start her campaign. Her work was very demanding, but on the whole was nowhere near as draining as her husband's job in the City. The stress levels were bad and weren't made any better knowing that the younger members of staff were snapping at his heels, wanting his position and prepared to do anything to get him out of their way.

At the drinks cabinet Alan's foot started tapping in time with the jazz Sophie had playing. He gestured towards her with the whisky bottle, she shook her head to decline a drink, and he replaced it with a flourish. She waited while he clinked two ice cubes into the glass then relaxed back in his armchair with a satisfied sigh.

"Do you remember me saying about Anthea getting married last spring?" she asked, wondering what level of attention he was prepared to give her that evening.

"Ah, yes. A lovely young couple, if rather idealistic. Have they sorted out a house yet or are they still living with her parents?"

A good sign, she thought. *He remembers the details and is showing interest.*

"Actually they've decided not to buy anywhere." She paused to check if he was still with her. "They've decided to start a world tour and have both resigned."

Alan chuckled. "A world tour? It sounds like a modern version of the Victorian Grand Tour. Very grand! How do

51

they think they can manage that in their impecunious state? Or have they found sudden musical fame?"

"They intend doing odd jobs along the way to eke out their funds – a bit of bar work, busking, obviously, that sort of thing - but basically that old camper van is going to be their home for the next year."

Alan snorted into his scotch, nearly choking. "What? That old heap? They'll only get as far as Calais and that's because the ferry will take them that far."

Sophie frowned at him. "Give them credit for some sense. It may still look ramshackle but they've done a lot of work to ensure it's mechanically sound." *Now or never, perhaps.* "Don't you think that's a glorious plan? To actually take the chance and follow your dream?"

Alan nodded. She could see from his unfocussed gaze he was remembering his own youthful wild dreams of freedom and adventure, but it wasn't long before the tension came back to his face. They'd been married long enough she could feel his joys, his pain and his sorrows. She knew he was also remembering life throwing restrictions and responsibilities at him, mostly before he was ready for them.

He sighed and shook his head. "Chance would be a fine thing indeed. It must be great to be young and free from care."

Sophie's heart went out to him. *Oh, my love, bear with me, keep listening, really listening, for a change.*

"You don't have to be young to follow a dream." She leaned forward and took his hand. "We're no longer young but we could still follow our dream. We've just had to be more patient than Anthea, that's all."

"What are you on about?" He sat up and grinned, play-punched her on the chin. "Have you been on the sherry, woman? I don't want a world tour!"

"No, darling, nor do I. I have a much more modest dream, and if you listen to your heart instead of your head I believe you'll admit it's your dream too." She paused, took her thimble off, then looked up, her eyes demanding his attention. "I want to move to Devon. It's not enough to go there each year on holiday for two weeks and then have to return here to work."

He laughed again. "Did you get through the whole bottle?"

"This isn't a joke, Alan. I'm serious." She gripped her sewing with both hands.

"Be sensible, Sophie. Without work we don't keep the bills paid each month."

"Sensible? I've been sensible all my married life and believe I still am being sensible." She got up and fetched the whisky bottle to top up his glass. "Think about it, Alan," she said as she poured. "Why do we need our high salaries?" She replaced the bottle and then sat down again, stroking the back of his neck as she passed. "Once we did, with a mortgage and family and all the high bills we faced here. But now? Why slave for those salaries when neither of us actually wants to be here any more?"

"But my career is here, everything I've worked for. I'd never find an equivalent position in Devon."

"Good!" Sophie was deliberately emphatic, slapping one hand on her sewing, then allowed her tone to soften. "You've done extremely well, darling, and I'm very proud of what you've achieved while we've been raising and supporting our family. But it's taken over your life. It's taken over our lives. The children have grown up now and I feel that not only have they left but you have, too. What about us? It feels like I'm facing a long prison sentence before you're forced to retire and we might get a chance to find some fun in life again. Alan, we don't have to wait!

We've done the youth and freedom bit, we've done the adulthood and caring for others bit. Now we're out the other side, at a new stage of our lives, one in which, yet again, there's only ourselves to consider."

"Aren't you forgetting Eddie?"

Their youngest son had moved out for a while. He was making noises about moving out again, but not really making much of an effort to do anything about it.

"I thought it was mothers who were supposed to come out with such concerns?" She smiled ruefully. "I know what you're thinking, wondering what the chances are that he'll want to scoot back home again." Sophie started sewing again while she talked. "Poor Anna, he didn't really give the lass much of a chance last time of building a relationship that could stand the test of time, did he? It was very wrong of him to expect her to cope with all the domestic details of life as well as hold down a job just as demanding as his own. He's very lucky she's prepared to give him a second chance, albeit with the rules more clearly defined. He needs definite parameters set."

She glanced up and saw the merriment in Alan's eyes. "And it's not my fault, Mr Cheshire Cat there, who had the privilege of the handmaiden bit because I was too besotted with you not to! I've tried to teach him how to be a modern man. I offered repeatedly to teach him to cook but all I get is, "I'd learn to cook if I wished to become a chef", and he still believes he'll be able to employ a domestic - on his salary? - never mind I've told him otherwise. He really is terribly self-absorbed, and a boring old fart to boot."

"Sophie!" Alan was quite shocked. "How can you speak about your own son like that?"

"Well he is! You have to admit that he does show extreme reluctance to let life show him the wonderful experiences that are on offer if only you are prepared to keep an open mind and a flexible attitude. Perhaps if we weren't here to pick up the pieces for him this time he'd be forced to give life a proper try. He is thirty after all – it's high time he left home for good. If he wants marriage then he has to take on the whole bag of responsibilities that go with it."

"OK, so working on the premise that it's just the two of us, what do you envisage us doing in Devon? Monthly bills, however much lower they are, still have to be paid, you know."

"Of course I know. What we would do is relax, like we do every year when we're on holiday there. You know I don't mean 'do nothing' by that: you can be very relaxed and still be working. It's all in the mind. We'd enjoy a quality of life that we're missing here in the South East. You know the expression – if you want to get out of the rat race, stop being a rat. Somewhere along the way we lost a reasonable work/life balance and I want it back."

"But -"

"Hold on! Hold on!" She stalled his attempted interruption with a hand raised against him. "Let me show you something."

Sophie reached for a file from her side table that Alan had assumed was more work she'd had to bring home.

"I feel like I'm being set up here."

Sophie was imperturbable. "Not at all. We both know that rational decisions cannot be based on anything other than hard facts."

"Which you've been busy gathering..."

"Wasn't it you who insisted I learn to walk around the wall to see what was on the other side rather than taking a flying leap?"

They smiled at each other, knowing that in their long marriage neither had ever taken a binding decision without the full knowledge and consent of the other. Their different approaches to life complemented and balanced each other beautifully.

"I have here a current valuation on our house and details of all expenditure that would be involved in settling our affairs here. I also have details of suitable properties in Devon in two categories – a potential home for us, and likely properties for holiday lets. The spreadsheet shows predicted income and expenditure over the course of the first year, projected for a further five years, for several of the possible combinations of purchases of said properties."

Alan took the folder thoughtfully but couldn't help laughing at the very first entry.

"Sorry love, but you've got your figures wrong here. £750,000 for our house? I think not!"

"Actually, that's a conservative figure. The desirability of this area has rocketed in recent years. Surely you've noticed the number of expensive new cars on the drives now, not the beat-up wrecks there used to be? We don't have local cafes, we have bistros. I used to be able to buy my knitting wool on the High Street: now I can spend £50,000 on a designer kitchen. Affluent people want to live here, and the competition has driven prices up. If you care to refer to the enclosed building societies' report that was published last week in the papers, you will see that for this area the forecast is for it to continue to increase at the rate of 2% a month for the rest of this year."

"We only paid £42,000 for it. These buyers must need their heads examined."

"But we won't insist on it if we are to be the beneficiaries of such madness." Her eyes twinkled sensing she might win him round. "Besides, we've spent a great deal on it over the years, extending and improving it."

The sheets in the folder were turned very slowly as the

56

dream started to gel into a real possibility in Alan's mind. He peered at her over the top of his glasses. "I notice you've selected older, rather run-down properties to choose from for our next home."

A shared look was sufficient for them both to be back in that time long ago when it had been their ambition to buy a house with character, one that was just about habitable but would need years of empathetic renovation to turn it into their treasured home. Back then, with a baby on the way, common sense had prevailed. They had compromised and bought somewhere that could be improved, and had been over the years, but was fully habitable from the outset. Most of their married life had been a compromise in one way or another.

"We're still relatively young, Alan. We can do this. And think how much more experienced we are with DIY now."

"Will we have any time left over from working on home and garden to still play golf together?"

She noticed he had said 'will we', not 'would we'.

"The final section of that folder details all the local courses," Sophie assured him smugly.

Alan went over to give her a kiss on his way to the drinks cabinet. "I'm glad it's such nice things you try to talk me into. But I need a replenishment to get over the shock."

The lounge door opened quietly. "Hello," Eddie said, and ambled over to the sofa.

Eddie had never been noisy, or gone in for boisterous play, or did anything in the way that other boys did. Sophie had never been able to understand him.

"Oh good, glad you're mending those first." Eddie indicated the jeans that lay in Sophie's lap. "Anna's insisting on going to the barn dance in the community centre near her place tonight. I tried to talk her out of it but no joy. With any luck that sagging old ceiling will have come down before we get there and save us all that sweating and stomping."

"Hello, love. Barn dances can be great fun. You'll have a lovely time together."

He didn't look convinced.

"I'll get your tea on in a minute, but there's something we'd like to discuss with you first."

As always, Eddie gave his mother his full attention. As always it was impossible for her tell what he was thinking.

"Your father and I have just decided to sell up and move to Devon."

"Move? Move when?" Eddie's face was expressive of his shock at the prospect, which really surprised his mother.

Alan removed some of the worried frown from his son's face when he interjected, "We don't know for sure yet. Your mother and I have only just started discussing it. We are agreed in principle but it could be many years yet."

"Oh, Alan, why wait?"

"Sophie, you said yourself that house prices here are still rising. There's a lot to be taken into consideration."

"Yes, we could continue to 'consider' ourselves into immobility!"

"And what about me?" Eddie asked. "I want a say in this too."

"Eddie, it won't affect you soon. You're getting married to Anna, remember? You're moving out anyway."

"Well actually, no, I'm not." He paused, his eyes flicking from one parent to the other. "I'm going to tell Anna tonight that I don't really think it's a good idea. We'll go ahead with the wedding plans and then both move in here. It will save us a small fortune."

Sophie knew how much Eddie brooded about things before making decisions. She realised he had probably been wondering how to break it to them for quite some time, and now the issue had been forced on him prematurely. His father's face confirmed for them both that this was not the best timing.

"I see." Alan didn't need any more ice to his scotch: his voice was sufficient. "You have the gall to believe you should have a say in what we do, but did not think that we should be asked for our consent to your plans? Plans which, I might point out, would have a major impact on our lives!"

"Dad! It's not like that at all!"

Sophie watched the blood suffuse his face. She was sure it was primarily embarrassment, but there was definitely anger there too. At last, some sign of real emotion from him.

"No? Tell me, what is it like? You plan to move in unannounced with your new bride, without our permission and with no indication of how long you intend staying. Or perhaps you expect to remain here hoping that possession is nine-tenths of the law when your mother and I die?"

"Alan!" Now Sophie was shocked. *What have I started here? Alan and Eddie have never had a cross word before and now they're all but at each other's throats.* She'd noticed more and more of late just how short Alan's fuse had become during the past year, how volatile his moods.

Eddie jumped up, his mouth working frantically while the brain was still disconnected. "You... you taught me to be financially prudent, to consider all the options, to... Stop looking at me like that! Oh! I'll speak to you later when you're calmer and more rational!" Eddie slammed the door on his way out.

"The insolent pup! Sophie – speak to the estate agents tomorrow. The Collingwoods are on the move, and young fellow me lad can like it or lump it!"

Oh dear, Sophie thought, *now I'm the one who wants to*

discuss the issue further. Good lord, Eddie - when Alan's 'calmer and more rational'? Whatever next? You'll never make progress that way. But I don't want a black cloud over your wedding day. Is the path to a dream ever smooth when a family's involved?

~~~

Something About Suzy

As I mature I hear 'beautiful' and 'elegant' more often than 'pretty' and 'dainty'. But I still hear, "All Salukis are gorgeous, but there's just something about Suzy, something special".

Mind, it wasn't always that way, oh no! Little do they realise the overpowering hatred and loathing I feel for The Man, the rage that threatens to spill over onto those who don't deserve it. All they see is my 'aloofness' as I back away because his height is the same, or his hair that same darkness that is not quite black.

It's not their fault, but as the revulsion shivers through me I am forced to create space between us. I can see how deeply they feel my blatant rejection of them. I know that everyone I meet now just wants to love and spoil me, but The Man poisoned all possibility of the easy acceptance of such adoration. Male hands are memories of the vicious blows I received, male feet of the labouring pain of breathing after another thoughtless kick to my ribs in his careless drunkenness.

I don't think he ever saw me for myself, just the status that the children I would soon be able to bear would bring him among his friends.

Friends? Scum! Scum! That was one opportunity for braggadocio I was determined would never be his. Owwwoooo! I can't help but howl - my brain and guts are pure acid and black bile as I think of him! Oh, it hurts! I can't help it! May he fall in the slurry pit, his last awareness be of filth sliding into his mouth and nose and lungs. He should rot in hell for all eternity! Owwwoooo! Owwwoooo!

-0-

It was difficult, but I was determined. I had to convince him of my passive submission to his will while maintaining a never-ceasing covert alertness, watching for my chance. It finally came during winter's last cold snap. He hadn't expected it after the warming breath of spring all week, so he wasn't dressed for it. On his return his cold fingers fumbled over the chains and his beer-blurred vision did not spot his mistake. Oh, it was so hard to wait until I was sure he was settled for the night! My heart was racing as I slipped away from the caravan towards the wood. Fear lent my feet speed even as I cried in panic, hearing his vicious mongrel of a guard dog voicing the alarm, lunging towards me and bringing The Man lumbering to the door.

Be still! Be still! Don't give him any clues. Oh, night's blackness, be kind to me.

He lurched against the doorframe, peering blearily into the darkness, the light behind him sending the shadow of my worst nightmares clawing towards me.

"Damn her! The bitch'll be back when she's cold enough and hungry enough."

Never! I'll die rather than go back to him. Hungry enough? I was always hungry: my worms took more benefit from my meagre rations than I ever did.

I was so badly malnourished and weak I was ill-equipped to survive by myself. My failing health made me slow, so slow that the authorities eventually caught me and forced me into care. Trapped again, but at least in this prison I wasn't beaten and half starved. I curled into a tight ball on my bed in the corner, trying to shut out the continual noise of my fellow prisoners. I just needed time to recover my strength then try again for freedom.

Unexpectedly, freedom arrived the very next day in a blue car. It was really strange. All She did was sit down and cuddle me in. We looked deep into each other's eyes, searching for the true messages from the soul, and I didn't feel trapped. I felt safe. I felt loved.

I'd never felt this elation of good emotions before, this soaring of spirit. Even the memories of my mother had been smothered in her feelings of despair, fear and danger. She knew from the start that her attempts to protect us were futile. But she gave me the will to survive! Because of her I had the determination not to be trapped, as she was, in a life sentence of male domination.

We have an oral tradition, passed from dams to pups, maintained over thousands of years. We know who we are, where we have come from. We know about our close association with humans, how we are bred to be the finest of partners in the hunt through the deserts for prey. The hawks do the spotting while we follow with our humans on horseback: we watch them then close in for the kill, thinking and acting independently but working together. We are not kelb, we are gifts from Allah.

But then? I was weak. I was frightened. I was alone.

I was desperate for love.

"She only came in yesterday," my Warder told Her, watching me curl into Her. "I've wormed her and the vet did her shots when he was here for another dog, but I haven't had chance to take her in to him to get the rest sorted. As you can see there's mange and an ear infection and both eyes infected too. But I'm really not set up here for her kind. We take the big dogs here mostly. I'm scared the pikeys will break in to get her back once they know she's here."

She pulled me in closer. "I'll take her now," She said and looked up at the Warder, daring him to gainsay Her. "I'll care for her. She'll be safe with me." She stroked me, careful not to touch the agonisingly painful ear. "We'll heal you," She told me. "You won't ever feel pain again if I can prevent it."

The couple took me to their home and persuaded me it was my home too, if I wanted it. If I wanted it? My feelings and desires were now important too! Home – the very word had had no real meaning for me before I met them. They taught me about home and family, about caring for each other.

Our first morning together I just curled into Her lap, Her love balm to my wounded soul. They made me well and allowed me to be a child again. You should see all the toys they bought me! We spent hours playing together, and then, even better, they decided I was lonely for my own kind and that it would be rather nice to give someone else a home too. So that's how I met Fleet. Now when we go out for walks together I have someone to run and play with. My Humans are OK, but you know what I mean.

Fleet's bigger and stronger than me. He loves me and is prepared to defend me if I feel threatened. In his eyes I'm always right, even when taking both offered treats, surreptitiously hiding one for later. He understands what I went through because his background is not dissimilar to mine, although his suffering, his neglect and abuse, originated in ignorance of our breed rather than evil intent. We are not lap dogs or dull-witted dogs. We can think for ourselves. We are sighthounds, with a proud heritage.

Fleet and I think the same way, we play the same way. When we run with the wind our plumed tails are our rudders, just as it was for our ancestors, hunting in the winds of the deserts. He cares for me and respects me. We work and play as a pair, indivisible.

There's the key in the lock – my Man's back from work. I spring up ready for the daily ritual of greeting, a ritual we both anticipate and enjoy.

"Hello, gorgeous! How's my girl today?"

He sits on the sofa with me while I make a big fuss of him. I know he's *a* man, but he's nothing like The Man. I feel bile in my throat again and push those black memories away. This man doesn't see me as a twice-yearly source of lurcher pups to sell for illegal hare coursing, abusing my royal Saluki heritage, draining my body until at just middle age I'd be a worn-out dried husk to be dumped as a worthless encumbrance. Anyway, he's my Queen's consort and I'll do anything to keep Her happy. If She wants me to show respect and affection for Her chosen partner then I shall.

A quick change of position is needed as Fleet comes over for his fuss. I use my body to edge him away sideways. It's still my turn, Fleet! I feel a bit disgruntled as he reaches over me to rub Fleet's silky ears, but then, and I know it's immature and unworthy, but I can't help gloating as I hear him say, "Hello, my boy. Yes, I love you too, but there's just something about Suzy."

~~~

Time Out

Lynn felt a bid of a fraud when her Mum's friends cooed over how good it was of her to give up part of her precious summer holiday before A level studies started to go and care for other people.

This is my chance of freedom, for goodness' sake! I'm doing it for me.

For the first time in her sixteen years of life she would be on her own, and was determined to show the world what was what. There'd be no parental restrictions, no nosey neighbours twitching their net curtains, and it wouldn't cost her a penny. Everything was paid for by the charity: travel, board, the works except for her personal entertainment during her free time. She was sure rotating eight hour shifts to give 24/7 care wouldn't be too bad, and that it would be quite interesting to experience being awake all night. And London was just a tube ride away. London had to be able to offer better entertainment than anything her village could even dream of. Lynn's only regret was that her best friend would not agree to go too, but Janice had her heart set on being a farmer's wife. She would not consider anything that might upset or worry Bill, heir apparent to the 150 acres closest to their homes.

Roll on Saturday! No farm's big enough to hold Lynn Reid back.

-0-

"Relax, love, I can't afford plastic surgery to remove all those frown lines," Brendon gently teased his wife.

Viv shot him a startled glance, the frantic clicking of her knitting needles ceasing abruptly. "I can't help but worry about her," she said. She dropped her knitting in her lap and ran her fingers through her short curly hair. "Why did Lynn have to choose the furthest Home from us? What if she needs us to get there quickly?"

"And why would she need us? She's only going for two weeks. Anyway, the Holiday part of the name refers to what the disabled guests are going for, not Lynn. Remember, most of them will be quite elderly, probably overweight and cranky, and Lynn will end up so exhausted by the end of every shift she'll be glad to just put her feet up with a cup of tea."

"Overweight? Oh no! What if they don't teach her how to lift properly? She could injure her back, be facing a lifetime of problems -"

"Darling, you know you checked out the charity thoroughly: not one injury, or complaint, or piece of scandal. There's a string of both guests and volunteer workers eager to go back, all giving glowing references. Qualified permanent staff are now in loco parentis so I, in loco doctoris, prescribe this for us."

Brendon smiled at Viv's wide-eyed childlike expression as he produced from 'nowhere' a venerable looking bottle of brandy. "A little something I came across on my way home from work," he murmured while taking down the Waterford crystal brandy balloons from the display cabinet.

"But it's Blue Butterfly!" Viv protested. "How could it be 'on your way home' when there's not an off-licence for miles around that's good enough to sell that?"

"Oh, you recognise it then?" Brendon queried with a twinkle in his eye.

Their shared memory of an enchanted evening on their honeymoon, when Brendon introduced Viv to the sensuous pleasure of a fine brandy, eased the tension of this evening nearly nineteen years later.

"All fledglings have to test their wings eventually. At least we have made this first flight as short and safe as we can."

-0-

What a weekend! What hard work! What fun! What interesting people! Wow! And as for Rob...

Lynn couldn't believe her luck when, that first Saturday after all the introductions had been made at the Meet and Greet party in the main lounge, she found herself allocated to Rob's shift. Rob was a permie and, in Lynn's opinion, an absolutely gorgeous hunk of manhood. Six feet two inches in his socks, broad shouldered and slim hipped, with soft expressive brown eyes and his lips – Lynn couldn't drag her eyes off them.

They'd look too full and sensuous on a bloke if it was anyone else. They're just begging for a fingertip touch, a kiss...

Of course all the women, young and old, were in love with him. He lifted Nellie in and out of her wheelchair as though she were a mere slip of a girl rather than the 18 stone paraplegic she actually was. His genuine interest and concern for everyone got the old biddies acting like simpering debutantes with their beaux. Rob flirted outrageously with them but also captivated the men with chats about cars, football, gardening, suggestions for the next chess move. Lynn was sure she knew where his interest really lay though. She'd noticed how he was always aware of where she was, the special shared glance each time their work brought them close.

Oh well, time to clock in with the parents. Best not to mention Rob again, perhaps.

She knew her Mum's imagination was liable to run

71

further on a few words than anyone else in England. She got up to go to her room for a bit more privacy while she made the call. Lynn softly sang the opening lines of a Foreigner track as she made her way through the high-ceilinged, sunny morning room of the Victorian manor house. *I want to know what love is, I want you to show me...*

As she passed, Rob glanced up at Lynn from the game of Jenga he was playing with two of the guests, and smiled that irresistible slow smile of his.

The weather had really helped boost the atmosphere of fun over the past few days. The trip to Southend with its ice creams on the front, and the wheelchair races they'd had around Croydon shopping centre, had been a really good laugh, but now it was time for her own fun. Her shift had finished at two that afternoon and as she wasn't due back on until six the following evening Lynn was looking forward to plenty of time in the city and a leisurely lie-in to recover from it. She wandered out into the garden in search of the others on her shift as they'd all agreed to go together. Sounds of laughter directed her steps to the swimming pool, where she found they were obviously nowhere near ready to go.

"Hi, Lynn," Cassie called. "Go and get your cossie, it's gorgeous here."

"We all agreed we were going to London this afternoon," Lynn protested, wincing at how petulant she sounded even to her own ears, but she hated the way the vibrant copper-haired Cassie always seemed to be centre stage without even trying.

"Oh, we can go to town any old time." Cassie dismissively waved one well-manicured slim hand. "It's not often we get such glorious weather though. Better make the most of it."

"Well, some of you may be able to go to 'town' any

time you like but some of us live hundreds of miles away!"

Lynn stormed off, even more annoyed that there wasn't even a pause in the laughter and splashing round the pool. *I don't need them to be able to enjoy myself. Watch out London, here I come!*

-0-

Rob's appearance at the French windows caused a clandestine rearranging of scantily clad bodies to ensure they showed to best advantage. He'd spent the afternoon catching up with laundry and housework in the flat he shared, as a member of staff, in the Home's extensive grounds. Now, as the heat of the day started to melt into the soft golden glow of evening he was looking forward to relaxing with Lord of the Rings in the garden. He'd heard there were plans to make a film trilogy and he'd decided he wouldn't watch them until he'd had a chance to remind himself of a story he hadn't read since he was a boy.

"Come on in," Cassie called. "The water's perfect."

"Only perfect with your fair presence in it, my lady," Rob bowed to her. He gracefully stripped his T-shirt over his head.

There was a collective intake of breath from the group, watching as the taut litheness of him flowed into a running header into the pool. Cassie squealed in mock terror, swimming to get away from the hands that reached for and caught her ankles, pulling her down into the sun-shaft brightness of the water. His deceptively lazy crawl soon powered him to the end of the pool and back. Several young pairs of eyes were glued to the flexing muscles that lifted him effortlessly back onto the edging lawn.

"I thought you were all going to town today," Rob commented.

"We couldn't leave you all lonesome, now could we?" Cassie said, looking up at him from under her eyelashes.

A quick glance round brought a small frown to Rob's brow. "Where's Lynn?"

"Oh, she huffed off by herself when we wanted to stay here."

The sudden hardness in Rob's eyes made Cassie wonder uneasily what she had done to offend him.

"Um... excuse me, ladies," Rob said after a slightly awkward pause. "There's, um, something I need to check on in the office."

None of their protests could dissuade him from grabbing a towel and hurriedly drying himself down as he headed back to the house.

Oh you sweet, naïve child. Please, God, protect her until I get there, Rob prayed, cursing his fingers as they fumbled on the catch of his crash helmet. He was unusually vicious kick-starting his beloved Triumph and the spurt of gravel left no doubt about just how much of a hurry he was in.

-0-

It's boring in London if you're on your own and don't know where to go, Lynn reflected morosely. Even the places of interest she had managed to find all seemed to cost a small fortune. She had stopped mentally calculating how many weeks it would take her to earn the various entry fees from her Saturday checkout job. A heavenly smell of freshly ground coffee beans had tempted her to enter a rather shabby café. She sat there, disconsolately nursing a latte. She tested this new name to herself – cafe latte - she had to get it right when she told Janice about London. She looked around, the corners of her mouth downturned. The only bright thing in the place was the gleaming, steaming, coffee machine, snorting exuberant steam at the cups.

Her seat in the window showed couples and groups of people pass, all of whom seemed to know how to have a good time. Stubborn pride alone kept her from catching the next tube back to the graceful manor and its peaceful gardens. She felt tired, dirty and deafened from the incessant noise of the city, a very insignificant mote in this throng of humanity, but she was not prepared to face the amused looks from Cassie and crew when she answered the inevitable questions should she return early.

One group didn't just pass by. It felt like a mini storm crashing through the door and noisily jostling past her table on their way to the counter. They all looked so happy, so together, so very obviously Londoners at home in their city.

"All right, sweetheart?" One of the lads winked at her in passing.

Lynn blushed furiously, ashamed to find her close scrutiny had been noticed. She wanted to crawl under the table out of sight. Then her attention was caught by their myriad orders. *Are there really that many different styles of coffee?* The group clustered on the tables next to hers and it became all too apparent how prim and proper her clothes and hairstyle were in comparison, how very obvious it was that she was no city girl.

"I'm Chas," the one who had winked at her called across. "What are you doing sat there all alone? You're far too beautiful to have been stood up. What's your name? You don't mind if I come and sit with you, do you? We're a bit crowded here." Fitting deed to word he straddled the chair opposite her. Oh where was the witty reply when she needed one?

"Leave her be, Chas," a blonde with amazing eye makeup chided him. "Can't you see you're embarrassing her?"

Lynn groaned mentally.

"Never mind them," one of the others consoled her. "Thinks he's God's gift, he does, and Babs was never high in the tact department."

"I'm Lynn," she managed to stammer. "This is my first trip to London." She could have bitten her own tongue off, hearing herself blurting that out.

"Yeah, we guessed that." Babs laughed and her friends joined in.

The noise level rose steadily and Lynn didn't know which part of the various conversations to listen to or join in with. Ultimately it was just too much for the owner. As other people showed signs of being put off staying, or even entering, he let his feelings be known.

"Oi, you lot, just keep it down will yer!"

"Yeah, yeah, yeah," Chas called back. "We know when we we're not wanted. Come on – let's go somewhere they like a bit of life."

"Oh," said Lynn. "Well, it was nice to meet you."

"Don't be daft! You're coming too."

Lynn knew she should say no, but what the hell, they were such good fun. What harm would it do?

-0-

Rob dialled the mobile number he'd jotted down from the office file, praying that it would not immediately switch him to message service. It rang, and rang... *Please, Lynn, come on, answer it, dammit!*

"Hello?"

He barely recognised the voice answering his call. *Keep it cool now, no need to frighten her.* "Lynn? Hi, it's Rob. Look, I changed my mind and came into town. Do you fancy meeting up for a bite to eat or something?"

"Rob!" she squealed in his ear. "Where're you?"

It didn't bode well to him that she was slurring so much.

"Never mind where I am – where are you? I've got the bike so I can come and meet you."

"Dunno..." She struggled to make her tongue behave properly. "Where are we?" she asked Chas. "My friend brought me out for some fun," she confided to Rob.

"The Pelican," Babs told her when Chas remained silent.

"It's a peclian, um," she paused to concentrate, "Pelican, Rob."

"The one on Coldharbour Lane?" He knew that was the 'in' pub with the teenagers at the moment and hoped he was guessing right. Hell, the whole of Brixton was popular because of the police experiment there of tolerance to drug users.

"I dunno – s'pose so."

"Just wait there, love, I'll be with you in about half an hour."

When he arrived, Rob's quick assessment of the situation showed action was needed, and fast. *Thank goodness the traffic's been relatively light.*

"You're upsetting the lady. I suggest you remove your hands from her before I remove them for you." Rob spoke quietly but the menace of his cold tones was evident.

"You and whose army?" Chas demanded, his voice loud in the sudden stillness. "This bitch has let me pay for her drinks all evening and now won't even give me a fucking kiss let alone a piece of that tight little arse."

He didn't even see the clenched right hand coming as it slammed into his jaw, jerking his head sideways as he crashed over the table.

"Does anyone else have any comment to make?" Rob asked coolly, drawing a sobbing Lynn to his chest.

"No mate, no," were the hurried confirmations as the

rest of the group drew back.

"Come on, Lynn," Rob soothed her. "We're going home."

-0-

Gary helped settle Lynn into the spare bed, then went to bed himself. Rob sat beside her, gently smoothing back her hair. He murmured comfort now that the first shuddering storm of weeping had passed. The realisation of the danger she had got herself into had hit hard.

And, oh boy, will she have a hangover tomorrow!

He had decided he'd better watch her during the night, just in case she vomited in her sleep or woke to night terrors.

"I love you, Rob," Lynn sniffed, the hiccuping sobs dying down as she slid towards sleep. "I'll always love you."

Rob smiled. "Just sleep now, we'll talk in the morning."

-0-

The curtains screeched a protest as Rob drew them. *Or is it really my head screeching?* Lynn screwed up her puffy eyes in protest at the light. *Is it really possible to feel this ill and not die?*

Rob placed a tray with coffee, tomato juice and toast on the bedside table. She groaned aloud.

"Come on now, you need to at least get some fluid inside you," Rob insisted. "Toast too would help, but I won't insist on it."

Sudden realisation dawned of where she was and what she had done to get there. *How humiliating!*

"Rob, I'm so sorry I've put you to all this trouble. I've

even taken your bed. I hope you weren't too uncomfortable last night? What's everyone going to say? What will they think?"

Rob decided she had to be told and sooner rather than later was probably best.

"Actually, you didn't take my bed. Well, it used to be, but Gary and I have a very comfortable double bed now."

He gave her a moment for this to sink in.

"You mean you're... you're..." *Oh no!*

"Gay?" Rob chuckled at the shock on her face. "Gary and I came out together shortly after we started work here. It's our second anniversary next week. It's a shame you won't be here for the party."

"He works here too? I've never seen around."

"No, he's manager of three Homes and has been away for a couple of weeks in the Welsh one."

A sudden memory of what she had said before sleep claimed her turned her face crimson. "Rob, about what I said last night -"

"What you said? When was that? I don't recall you saying anything." He tried not to laugh as Lynn dragged the sheet up over her head, grateful but totally mortified.

-0-

"There you go, Lynn." Her Dad patted her thigh as she sat in the passenger seat of the family car. "Go on, I'll park the car and see to your bags while you go and tell your mother about your great time away."

She kissed his cheek and ran to the kitchen where she knew her Mum would be preparing one of her favourites for tea to welcome her back.

"Hi, Mum!" she called. "The wanderer returns. Mmmm, that smells good."

79

"Hello, love. Well, was the world ready for my daughter?"

Lynn thought about just how ready the world had been to eat her up and spit her back in little pieces. *But it won't catch me on the hop next time.* She grinned and leaned over for a big hug.

"No, Mum, nowhere near ready for a daughter of yours. But it's good to be home."

~~~

Spirit Passing

The phone rang at the lowest time of night – 3am – when the mind and body of even the healthiest individual needs dragging back to consciousness.

"It won't be long now," Ruth told me calmly. "I know you wanted to be here with her."

"Yes, thank you." I spoke softly, glancing across at Neil, hoping we hadn't disturbed him. "I'll come straight away."

I eased myself out of bed and crept over to the chair where I'd dumped my clothes. I fumbled to sort them out in the darkness, couldn't make sense of them. Frustration simmered that such a simple task had suddenly become so hard. In trying to hurry I caught my foot in a tangled trouser leg and nearly fell, rattling the wardrobe door when I leant on it.

"Wha..?" Neil's sleepy voice halted my struggles. He raised himself on an elbow. "Mandy?" He turned on the bedside light. "Is it... now?"

I nodded and bit my lip. "Ruth's just called. I'm going over."

"Do you want me to drive you? Do you want me there too?"

I shook my head, let it droop forward so that my hair swung across my face and he wouldn't see how close to tears I was. "No, I'll be fine." I didn't think I could bear his sympathy, not just now. And I wanted Gran to myself.

I managed to finish dressing without mishap now the light was on.

"Go back to sleep, Neil." I went over and kissed him.

"I'll call if I won't be back before you go to work."

I started to turn away but he caught my wrist. "Promise me," he demanded. "Drive carefully, and call me if you need me." He cupped my face and ran a thumb across my lips. "Love you, babe."

I hugged him, accepting the strength he was offering. I almost changed my mind about wanting him there too, but I turned his light off and went to the bathroom.

I blew my nose, hard, and stared at my reflection. I looked scared. I splashed my face with cold water, ran the brush through my hair, then ran down the stairs to my car. At least traffic would be light, this early in the morning.

I had known the nurses would remember to phone me. In the weeks I had been visiting I'd got to know several of them quite well. They seemed to understand more than most people about what is important to people in life, probably because in the hospice they saw so much death. Gentle, accepting deaths mostly, thanks to modern analgesia and psychological support. Some still 'raged against the dying of the light', and nearly all of them still cried at times, privately, but somehow it was easier there to accept that death was a natural part of life. Overall it was a very busy, positive, bustling place. Even children enjoyed their visits to relatives, with plenty of activities going on which they were encouraged to join in. Only in their very final stages were patients to be found in bed.

As Gran now was.

Familiar roads by day took on a whole other nature by night. Lights bled in the rain, reflected shakily in puddles. My car stole through the eerily empty streets and the world held its breath, waiting for me to arrive.

Ruth saw me push open the swing door to the ward. She came over and nodded towards Gran's door.

"It's OK, Mandy, she's still with us." She smiled gently

and touched my arm.

I suppose she'd seen my expression on the faces of many relatives, the mixed fear and hope – am I in time? I went in and pulled a chair up beside her. Her hand was dry and cool, the wrinkled skin loose, tissue thin, bunching with no resistance beneath my rubbing thumb.

"Hello, Gran."

I'd thought about this moment many times. What was one supposed to say in the last minutes before someone you loved so much dies? I still didn't know the answer. Mine would be the last words she ever heard. Writer's block was nothing compared with the emotions stilling my tongue. My blank sheet of A4 stretched for hundreds of pages.

I leaned over to turn on the CD I'd compiled of some of her favourite music. Those wonderful opening bars of The Blue Danube sounded loud in the hushed room and I quickly turned the volume low. As the tantalising three notes rising through the octave led into the dance I raised my arms and my body swayed.

"We used to waltz together to this around the dining table."

The beds were quite wide so I slipped off my shoes and climbed up beside her, my head next to hers on the pillow. In her prime she'd been a big woman, a strong physical barrier between me and a frightening world, but there was little left of her now.

"Do you remember when I was little and stayed with you the first time? And the house creaking in the night scared me?" I whispered directly into her ear. "I untucked the blankets at the bottom and crept into your bed, up between you and Grandad. Grandad snorted in his sleep which made me giggle, and you rolled over and cuddled me in."

Now I was big, and she was small, so it was my turn to

cuddle her in.

"I was your special little girl and you both spoiled me rotten. It was wonderful. My own variety packs of cereals for breakfast, Viennese whirls in the afternoon, dunking my custard creams in your tea. Every year we went to the pantomime, and to see the Christmas displays in town. Special trips to London for the museums. Hours spent 'helping' you in the house and Grandad in the garden – you were so patient. My contributions must have made every job take twice as long, but it was an excellent apprenticeship. I still remember how to scale fish and prune apple trees, and I still peel fresh silver pennies for my winter vases. Every task I do at home brings you both to mind. Perhaps it's true that we don't really die while someone remembers us. Is that how you managed to keep going when Grandad died?"

The memories were flooding back. The years disappeared in my mind and I was a child once more.

"Not that I got it all my own way." I chuckled. "You sure knew how to give a tongue lashing when it was deserved, like the time I found your knitting and it was so fascinating watching the wool bobbling in and out I'd undone nearly a whole jumper front before you caught me! Or the time I snuck the kitchen scissors out of the drawer and made a big pile of tiny hyacinth florets on the table, leaving bare stalks in the pot. Why did that seem such a good idea at the time?

"But there was once – do you know it still hurts that you didn't believe me? I can still feel that sense of injustice as though it was just yesterday, when you accused me of ignoring you struggling home from the bus stop, laden with shopping, and not going to help you. I truly was totally oblivious of you while I sat on the garden gate. I was imagining travelling with that train that had just gone by.

Isn't it stupid that something from all that time ago still bothers me? Anyway, I hope you can hear me and maybe you believe me this time."

I brushed her thin white hair back off her forehead and kissed her cheek. I was pleased she still smelled of Camay and lily of the valley talc, just as she always had.

"It wasn't just my childhood, either. The teenage years would have been much tougher without you to sound off at. I even apologised to Mum a few times because you'd made me see things differently. Not that you said much. You just let me talk myself in circles until the truth dawned. Not that it always worked. Mum and I still have a way to go before we can put some of those rows, the things we screamed at each other, behind us for good.

"I don't suppose my first year at university helped. I know I was behaving totally outrageously. In fact I was a real bitch, wasn't I – so self-centred and egotistical. I thought I had all the answers and I knew nothing. It's not surprising Mum and Dad were ready to disown me.

"You were getting it from both sides. You must have wanted to knock our heads together. But you believed in me. You knew I'd work it out and come good in the end. All you did was give me that money. 'Promise me you won't spend it on anything else', you said. 'I've checked and it's enough for you to get back here from London, with a bite to eat on the way. You should never be afraid of adventures, but whatever happens in life you should always be able to get back home.' When I moved back to live here you said I could now spend that money on something nice for myself. I didn't, though. It's still in the little zip part of my purse. It's my talisman, see? As long as I have it I know I'll get home safe and sound. That would have made you cross if you'd known, wouldn't it? A granddaughter of hers superstitious!"

The CD track changed. "Can you hear that, Gran?" I sang along to Moonshadow, wishing she could sing it with me one last time. "And if I ever lose my eyes, weee..eee..ell, I won't have to cry no more.

"Saying goodbye is really hard, you know? I know it's the right time for you, but what will I do without you? I love Neil, he's a good man, but I can't talk to him like I do to you. You understand me so well I don't have to explain a lot of stuff: you already know what I'm going through. And as for Mum – well I reckon we're too much alike, too close, to be able to talk like you and I did. Perhaps it was that degree of separation between us that contrarily made us so close.

"Oh, Gran... How will I manage?"

I stopped talking, gave myself time to force back down the incipient tears. Now was not the right time for that. I rested my chin on her shoulder and leant my head against hers.

"That sounded really selfish, didn't it? Me, me, me! You taught me better than that. I hope I'll be able to teach my daughter the things that you taught me. Important things, like never letting anyone else decide things for me, like being able to face fear and do it anyway, like cherishing each and every moment. I've been late for no end of appointments because of you! You were right, though, about allowing ourselves the time to stand and stare, to drink in the unexpected moments of sublime beauty that will never come again in quite the same way. Feed your soul, you told me, because that's the only thing left at the end.

"Now here we are, at the end, and your soul is rich and healthy."

The gentle strains of Enya's On Your Shore were playing when Gran smiled, breathed out a soft sigh, and was gone.

How was it that I felt that moment? How did I know so immediately that it was now just an empty husk, so diminished by the years, lying on the bed in my arms? 'Vital signs' they called them, the indication of the difference between so much flesh and a living, breathing, person capable of all the emotions we revel in and suffer. Life's miracle and death's release.

I got up, ready to leave. Our last time together was over, Gran was no longer on that bed. I respectfully crossed the hands of her mortal remains across her chest, knowing the essence of Gran would always be safe in my keeping.

Then I, too, smiled as I felt the very first flutterings of the life in my womb. My hand crept down to my belly, protective of that new, precious soul.

"You're right, Gran - nature doesn't do straight lines, it's all circles."

~~~~~~~~~

~~~

~

Novels by Jay Howard

Changes:
Book 1 Never Too Late
Book 2 New Beginnings
Book 3 Past and Present - due for publication in 2013

About Jay Howard

Jay currently lives in Somerset, which she considers to be a gem among English counties. She has lived and worked in many places in England, Wales, Alberta and British Columbia. Holding dual citizenship through her father, who was born in Toronto, a visit to her 'other country' included a stay in her father's city followed by the four day train journey to the West coast. She describes the trip as 'the only way for an English visitor to start to comprehend the vastness and diversity of this land'.

Whilst admitting that trying so many different areas of work may not be ideal for most people, Jay believes that her experiences have given her insights that enrich her writing. She describes writing as 'enormously enjoyable and satisfying, but second only to golf in the level of frustration that must be endured to achieve the desired goal'.

18928719R00049

Made in the USA
Charleston, SC
28 April 2013